J

Eric Walters

orca soundings

ORCA BOOK PUBLISHERS

National Library of Canada Cataloguing in Publication Data

Walters, Eric, 1957-
Juice / Eric Walters.

(Orca soundings)
ISBN 1-55143-351-6

I. Title. II. Series.

PS8595.A598J93 2005   jC813'.54   C2005-900338-3

Summary: When a new coach comes to their school, Michael and his
teammates are convinced that steroids are the way to compete.

First published in the United States, 2005
Library of Congress Control Number: 2005920402

Orca Book Publishers gratefully acknowledges the support for its
publishing programs provided by the following agencies:
the Government of Canada through the Department of Canadian
Heritage's Book Publishing Industry Development Program (BPIDP),
the Canada Council for the Arts, and the British Columbia Arts Council.

Cover design: Lynn O'Rourke
Cover photography: Eyewire

Orca Book Publishers
PO Box 5626, Stn. B.
Victoria, BC Canada
V8R 6S4

Orca Book Publishers
PO Box 468
Custer, WA USA
98240-0468

08 07 06 05 • 5 4 3 2 1

Printed and bound in Canada.
Printed on 30% post-consumer recycled paper,
processed chlorine free using vegetable, low VOC inks.

For those who know that when
you play the game fairly, you win,
no matter what the score is.

Chapter One

"Everybody shut up and listen!" Dave yelled.

The huddle fell silent, but the noise of the crowd rolled out of the bleachers and washed across the field. I'd never heard a crowd so loud. Then again, I'd never played in front of this many people, or in this big a game. There were thousands and thousands of people, and everybody was yelling and screaming and cheering like crazy.

"I need everybody to focus!" Dave said. "Forget about the crowd, forget that this is the most important game any of us are probably ever going to play in. Forget about everything except what's going to happen on this field in the next half a minute."

Dave was the co-captain of the team. A senior and the strong safety, he called all of our defensive plays.

I looked past him to the big scoreboard at the end of the stadium. There were thirty-one seconds left and we were up fourteen to twelve. That was good. The problem was that they had the ball on our twenty-seven yard line. The bigger problem was that all twelve of their points had come from their field goal kicker. The biggest problem was that he hadn't missed from this distance all season.

It was awful to think that we could lose even though we hadn't let them get into our end zone to score a touchdown. We were going to lose to some scrawny little kid named Luigi, who couldn't have weighed more than a 120 pounds. Some kid who'd never even seen a football game before his family moved here from Europe last summer. Maybe he still didn't understand the game, but he could kick a football like nobody's business. I'd heard that there were college scouts in the crowd who'd come from around the country just to see him play.

"Moose, are you listening?" Dave barked.

I startled back to reality. "Of course I'm listening," I mumbled through my mouth guard.

"We're going to blitz," Dave said.

"Who's going to blitz?" one of the corners asked.

"Everybody."

"What?" somebody gasped. "You're joking, right?"

"Does this seem like the time for a joke? I want everybody to blitz."

"But if we all blitz, then the quarterback just has to lob a little pass to a receiver and he's gone for a touchdown."

"He's not thinking about passing," Dave said. "He's going to take the snap, spin around and hand off to a back who is going to try to move the ball into the very center of the field to set up the winning field goal."

"How can you be so sure about that?" the other corner asked.

"I'm not. What I am sure of is that we have to push them back or they'll get a field goal. We have to gamble. If I'm right, we win. If I'm wrong, we lose—losing by one point or losing by five is still losing," Dave explained, and it all made perfect sense.

"And if you get your hands on the ball carrier, don't tackle him to the ground. Hold him up and try to punch the ball free. Understand?"

Everybody grunted out agreement.

"Okay, break!" Dave yelled.

I started for the line. Everybody settled into their spots.

"Moose!" Dave called out and I stopped. He walked up and put his mouth right by the ear hole of my helmet. "They can't double or triple you on this play. Drive straight and hard for the hole—the moose is on the loose."

I smiled and nodded my head and he tapped me on the side of my helmet.

He was right. All through the game I'd been having to battle two offensive linemen. They'd been double-teaming me on every play—except for the times I'd found myself battling through three men.

That had been happening more and more throughout the season. In the beginning, nobody knew who I was, but as my sack total kept rising, I got more attention. Today all I'd managed was a few tackles, a couple of quarterback rushes and a shared sack. My arms were sore and my legs were heavy. It felt like I'd been running through water all day.

I also felt like I was letting my teammates down. The Moose hadn't been able to break loose all game. That could change with one play. Just one play.

I stood over my spot and waited as the other team's huddle broke and the players got into position. They looked confident, cocky. But why shouldn't they? All they had to do was hold onto the ball and make the game-winning field goal.

If Dave was right, they were going to hand off the ball to the back. He would cut along the line, right in front of me, to get to the middle of the field. The only thing between him and me was his offensive line. All I had to do was listen for the snap, explode off the line, knock down my man and probably another, and... Wait a minute, what if I hesitated for a split second? What if I waited for them to see the blitz coming from everywhere and then shot into the gap? The gap that would form when they left to try to cover the extra men?

"Three-ninety-eight!" yelled out their quarterback.

I felt the hairs on my arms stand up. This was the play that was going to decide the season, decide who would be champions.

"Three-ninety-eight. Hup. Hup. Hup!"

There was an explosion of sound and fury as both lines surged forward and bodies collided. I stutter-stepped and then shot through the little opening between two players, splitting them, practically untouched. I was suddenly standing in the backfield with the quarterback just off to the side! I launched myself at him as he turned to hand the ball off to the running back. My helmet hit his back with a sickening thud. I wrapped my arms around him, and the ball shot free and into the air! It bounced against the back's hands and then up and off his helmet and soared into the air. It was like I was watching in slow motion as the ball turned, end over end, hitting first one player and then another until it hit the ground and rolled and wobbled right into my outstretched hands. I pulled the ball toward me until it was right against my chest, protected, shielded and cradled there as bodies piled on top of me. It was mine.

Chapter Two

The dressing room was filled with sounds
and smells and emotions. Cheering, screaming, swearing, yelping. People chasing each
other around the room, spraying soda that
they'd shaken up. Lots of laughing. Some
were even fighting back tears. Tears of joy.
A few of the guys had stripped down to their
boxers and others were still in full uniform,
as if they thought that when they took off
their uniform, the party would end, or we'd

have to give back the trophy. The championship trophy. Saying that made me smile. Champions.

In the center of all the confusion and celebration stood Coach Reeves. He'd hugged each player as we came into the dressing room. He'd been in tears. Big tears. He hadn't been trying to hide them. I think he was still crying, but those tears had been lost in the tons of soda that had been sprayed all over him, soaking him from head to toe.

I sat off to the side, my back against the wall, drinking it all in. This was like a dream. Not just today, not just winning the championship, but the whole season. Me, Michael the Moose, making the senior team, then becoming a starter and then becoming more than a starter—becoming a star. I had to smile. I wouldn't say it to anybody else, but I had been one of the most important people on the team. I was the Moose. I'd led the team in sacks. And when I tossed down a quarterback, the stands would erupt, everyone making moose noises and yelling out "The Moose is on the loose, the Moose is on the loose."

I still cradled the football in my arm. I'd held onto it on the field and I hadn't let it out of my hands after the game. I knew that eventually I'd have to let go of it, but not yet.

"Could I have your attention!"

It was Coach. He was standing on a chair, waving his arms above his head. Slowly the noise and activity faded until all eyes were on him and the room was silent.

"This is all unbelievable," Coach Reeves said. "Unbelievable, but in another way, totally believable. How could we not win with this amazing group of individuals?"

Everybody cheered and clapped until he raised his hands. The noise died away.

"First things first. I need to award a ball. Where is the ball?"

I stood up and held it out.

"Toss it here, Michael," he said.

Coach was pretty well the only person besides my mother who called me Michael. I pitched him the ball.

"What I should do is cut this ball up into thirty-two pieces because everybody was the player of the game."

Part of me agreed, but another part felt disappointed. I thought that maybe he was going to give the ball to me. I had made the sack and recovered the ball. I'd saved the game, but that was okay. Whatever Coach said was okay. If he wanted to give the ball to somebody else, if he wanted me to eat the ball, I would have done it. It was only fair considering all that he'd done for us, what he'd done for me.

"But I'm not going to cut this ball up," Coach Reeves said. "It's too special. I am going to give it away. I'm going to give it away to the player who most represented what made this team so special, who brought us all the way to the championship game and then won that game. Before the game I met with my co-captains, and we all agreed that that honor should go to one player." He paused. It felt like everyone in the room was holding his breath. "Michael, could you please come forward."

My heart leaped into my throat. Had I heard him wrong?

"Way to go, Moose!" somebody yelled. Everybody started to cheer.

I jumped to my feet and stumbled forward. My teammates patted me on the back and cheered and continued to scream out my name.

Coach gave me a big hug. "Congratulations, Michael. You deserve this," he whispered in my ear. He handed me the ball.

"I really don't need to explain this decision to anybody in this room, but I am going to anyway. In my twenty-seven years of coaching, this is the first time that the most valuable player on the team wasn't a graduating senior. Michael, you are a player who improved with every game, who played with heart, who never quit and never let anybody else quit. You are why this team is a champion!"

Everybody started cheering again and the coach gave me another hug. I had to bite down on the inside of my mouth to keep myself from crying. I didn't want them to see me cry. I was Michael the Moose, football star, not blubbering baby.

"I have one more announcement to make," Coach said, silencing the crowd. I moved away, grateful that the attention was off me again.

"I've been coaching football at our school for twenty-seven years."

"Don't you mean one hundred and twenty-seven years?" somebody yelled out to a round of laughter.

Coach Reeves laughed too. "Sometimes it feels like that long. Twenty-seven years ago, in my first year as coach, our team captured the Division Two championship. I was young and just figured that we'd win every year. Now, twenty-seven years later, it seems fitting that we should win again—in my last year of coaching."

There was a gasp. I couldn't believe what I'd just heard him say. It couldn't be right.

"I've been thinking about this all year. I didn't want to say anything until after the game because I didn't want to have anything interfere with your focus." He reached up and brushed away some tears. "I qualify for my pension in June. I've been coaching, and teaching, for a long time. There's probably never a good time to say goodbye.

I've enjoyed every moment of every year, maybe none as much as this year. As most of you graduate this year and move on to college or go out and get a job in the real world, I'll be moving on too. It's just that most of my moving will be back and forth as I sit in a rocking chair on my front porch. I think I've worked hard enough to deserve a break!"

"Way to go, Coach!" somebody yelled out.

"You're the best!" somebody else screamed and everybody started cheering.

"Thank you all, so much. I'm hoping that all of you will come by, knock on the door and share a glass of lemonade with me."

"How about a beer?" somebody called out.

"Do you mean root beer?" Coach asked. Everybody laughed.

"I guess the big question, especially for those who are returning, is, who will coach you next year?"

"Yeah, who?" asked Caleb, one of our receivers, my best friend and one of the eleven of us who were returning the next year. He sounded as anxious as I felt.

"You don't have to worry about that. I wasn't leaving you until I found the right replacement. You'll be guided by Coach Kevin Barnes."

For some reason that name sounded familiar.

"You mean Coach Barnes from Central?" somebody asked.

Coach Reeves nodded. "Yes. Coach Barnes from Central. The coach who has led his school to four Division One championships in the past five years. You're trading up to a newer and better version."

"Maybe newer but couldn't be better," Dave, our co-captain, said.

"We're lucky to have him come to our school," Coach said. "It's very rare for a coach, especially one as successful as him, to move to a smaller program. I guess it means that he's not just a smart coach, but smart enough to realize that he's moving to the best school in the whole country. He's lucky to have you kids to coach—the best kids."

He stopped and wiped away some more tears with the back of his hand. I was closer to tears then ever.

"Now I want you all to put away those sad faces. This isn't a funeral. This is a celebration. A celebration of the best team I ever coached—the champions!"

Everybody started cheering again, but not me. It wasn't a funeral, but it did feel like I'd lost more than I'd gained.

Chapter Three

I hated hearing my name over the school PA system. I liked to just sit at the back of the class and be left alone. I knew I wasn't being called for doing anything bad—especially since I was supposed to go to the gym office and not the main office. Still, I liked being in the background more. That was hard these days. Everywhere I went, kids knew who I was. Heck, everywhere I went in town it seemed like everybody knew who I was—I was the Moose. In a town like ours, football was everything. If you were a star, then people knew who you were. And suddenly, being the Moose meant I was a star.

Funny, I'd been called Moose since I was in grade one. Some stupid kid, whose name I didn't even remember, had said that my hair stuck up like I had antlers. That, combined with the fact that I was the biggest kid in the class—I was always the biggest kid in the class—got me the nickname Moose. For years I hated it because it wasn't meant as a compliment. It was like being a big, dumb, clumsy moose who tripped over his own feet. Since I'd started playing football, it had become something different. I was The Moose. The big, not-so-clumsy, not-so-dumb kid who could run over the opponents—run over them like a Moose—and get to the quarterback or the running back. The guy who could flatten a fullback like a pancake. And whenever I made one of those plays, everybody on the field, everybody in the stands, would yell "The Moose is on the Loose," and the school band would start playing. I wasn't so clumsy anymore, and my hair was as short a buzz cut as you could get without shaving your head.

"Hello, Moose," a girl said as I passed by.

"Um…hi," I stammered.

"Great game," she said and flashed me a big smile.

I didn't know who she was. I think she was in grade nine or ten. Lots of people who knew me, I didn't know. Caleb said that I had to start taking advantage of that. Caleb was always better at talking than me. He was a lot better than me at a whole lot of things—especially things related to school. He just breezed through classes, getting nineties. I had to work like crazy to keep my marks in the seventies.

I turned and watched the girl walk away. I'd be more than willing to have Caleb work something out with her.

I turned the corner. Caleb was standing by the gym office door. There were five other guys, all in our grade, all on the football team. Caleb waved.

"How you doing, Moose?" Caleb asked.

"Not bad. How about you, Squirrel?" Caleb hated that nickname and I only called him that occasionally to bug him.

"Man, how come you get the good nickname?" he asked.

"Don't look at me," I said. "I didn't hang that name on you."

Caleb was smaller than me. Actually, everybody was smaller than me. And because we hung around all the time and I was called Moose, somebody started to call him Squirrel. From that cartoon, *Rocky and Bullwinkle*—squirrel and moose.

While we were standing talking, the rest of the returning ball players arrived.

"Anybody know what this is about?" I asked.

"Duh…football."

"I meant why are we meeting now, today?"

"I just figure anything that gets me out of Spanish has to be good," Caleb said.

Almost on cue I heard Coach's door open and I spun around. It wasn't Coach. It was a man dressed in a fancy suit, his hair all slicked back.

"Please come in," he said as he motioned for us to enter the office. We shuffled in through the open door. I expected Coach to be inside. He wasn't there either.

"Please sit," the man said and we all took seats.

"I'm sorry to take you out of classes, but I needed a chance to introduce myself. I'm Coach Barnes, your new coach."

I was hoping we'd meet him, but I figured it wouldn't happen until school started in the fall. With that suit and hair he didn't look like a coach—well maybe a coach in the NBA. He walked over until he was standing directly in front of one of the guys.

"I'm pleased to meet you," he said as he stuck out his hand to shake.

"I'm pleased to meet you. My name is—"

"Your name is Robert Erickson, if I'm not mistaken."

"Yeah, that's me," Robbie said. "How did you know?"

"I know lots of things. I know you're a cornerback. You started half the games this season but you had problems with a knee injury. I know you're fast and hard to beat on fly patterns. I know you had an eighty-seven in math but almost failed English. I know you live with both parents and you have seven older sisters." He shook his head. "You poor boy. With that many girls in the house, do you ever get to see the inside of a bathroom?"

Everybody laughed.

"I know lots about everybody." He walked down the line, introducing himself to each player, saying who they were, what position they played, something about their family and their school marks. Finally he stood in front of me.

"You're Michael Monroe. The Moose. You play tackle. You came from being a second stringer on the junior team last year to lead the team in sacks and tackles. You were the MVP for the season. You live with your mother and you have no brothers or sisters. You do well in school with a consistent average in the mid-seventies. So how am I doing?"

"Good. I mean right...about me and everybody else."

"That's good to hear. As coach, it is my responsibility to be right about everything all the time. I even know something about you that you don't know," he said, pointing at me.

"You do?"

"Yes. I know you're going to be the hub of our entire defense. I also know that I'm standing here talking to one of the team's captains."

"Me? You want me to be one of the captains?" I gasped. The rest of the guys started clapping.

"I see they agree with my choice. You look surprised, Moose."

"Well..."

"After the way you played this year, there was no other choice. Didn't you think this might be a possibility?"

"I was sort of hoping, but whoever you named would be okay."

"That's the sort of attitude that your old coach told me about when he recommended you for the spot. He said you were a leader both on and off the field. He said that there was nobody who was willing to work harder, to sacrifice to get the job done."

I felt like I was going to start to blush. I looked down at my feet.

"And when the offense is on the field, there will be two other captains on the field." He turned to face Caleb. "The Squirrel is going to be one of the other captains."

"Wow, cool, great!" Caleb exclaimed, and everybody, including me, clapped and cheered.

"Obviously two popular choices. My third captain isn't even in this school yet. He's a transfer student who will be starting in the fall."

"Somebody new is moving to town?" Robert asked.

"Expect a couple of transfers. He might even be living with me," Coach Barnes explained.

"You have a son?"

"I have two sons. One in grade two and the other in grade four. The older one has a heck of an arm, but I think he's still a little young to be on the team. Sometimes my wife and I take in players with potential but a troubled home life. It's my way of giving back. But right now it's time for a tour of the school."

"Sure, we can show you around," Caleb said.

"No, I'm going to show you around," Coach Barnes said.

"But we already know our way around here," Caleb said, voicing the confusion that the rest of us were feeling.

"I'm sure you know everything that is here. I'm going to show you what is going to be here. Come."

Chapter Four

We followed Coach Barnes out of the office and into the change room. He stopped and we all gathered around.

"This is your change room. Your old change room. By the time you return in the fall, this will be completely redone. It will be repainted. The lockers will be replaced with bigger ones. Ones that lock. Up there, one in each corner, there will be speakers to go with our new sound system. It will be incredible. Music helps to create mood, a winning mood."

He walked over and opened up the door to the equipment room. The stink of stale air, sweat and mold came flowing out.

"This will be redone. There will be a massage table in that corner. I've arranged for a therapist to come out twice a week to treat your strains and injuries." He turned to Caleb. "You know that hamstring injury that kept you out of three games this year? With the proper treatment you could have been back in one."

"That would have been great," Caleb replied. "I didn't know massage could make that big a difference."

"It can when you combine it with whirlpool treatments. That's what's going to be in the other corner—a new whirlpool tub."

"Wow."

"Unbelievable," I muttered to myself.

"A winning team starts in the dressing room. Come."

We followed him into the girls' change room. That felt strange, but he had to know what he was doing. "This is being converted to an equipment and conference room."

"Where will the girls get changed?" I asked.

"I don't really know," he said. "That's not my worry. Oh, by the way, all of the football equipment, from sweaters to pads to cleats to jocks, will be brand-new. I arranged for us to be sponsored by a major manufacturing company that will remain nameless for now. In the back corner will be the conference area. Computer and projection system so that we can look at game film, do analysis and simulate plays. You're going to be impressed with the software that's available."

I couldn't help but think about Coach Reeves using a blackboard and a piece of chalk.

"This wall will have a gigantic refrigerator that will hold ice and cold drinks. Water, power drinks, protein drinks. You name it and it'll be there. It will be fully stocked all the time. Not just for games, but always, for any member of the team."

"That's amazing," Caleb said.

"But who's going to pay for all of this?" another one of the players asked.

"All taken care of. I have contacts, people who are willing to provide sponsorship in exchange for being involved with a winning program. But wait, the best is yet to come."

Caleb and I exchanged surprised looks. What could be better than all of this?

We trailed Coach Barnes out of the dressing room, down the hall and into the weight room.

"You gentlemen probably spend a lot of time in here," he said.

"Some of us more than others," I said, shooting Caleb a dirty look. He was always finding ways to avoid weights.

"All of the equipment in this room will be replaced. Everything."

"Everything?" I questioned. I'd spent so much time in here that some of the equipment felt like family members.

"Everything. The stuff in here is from a different century. Each station will have its own separate sound system, with headphones, and in all three corners there will be a television set. A forty-two-inch, flat-screen, high-definition television."

"My set at home isn't that big," Robbie exclaimed.

"You may come to think of this as your second home," Coach Barnes said. "Because if we're going to be successful, you are going to have to spend a great deal of time in here."

"You install a bed and I'll move in here right away," Caleb joked.

"And you have people who will pay for all of this too?" another one of the players asked.

"Sponsors and the school. One of the conditions of me coming here was that they had to bring everything up to date. To create the best product you have to have the best ingredients and the best tools. Nothing but the best is what they promised me."

He walked over to the far end of the weight room. He pulled a black marker out of his pocket and began writing on the white block wall! In big numerals he wrote "4" and then

"37" and finally "2." He turned back around to face us.

"Does anybody know what these numbers mean?" Coach Barnes asked.

We all looked at each other and then at him.

"The winning numbers in the lottery?" somebody finally asked.

"You're half right. They are the winning numbers, but they have nothing to do with the lottery."

He circled the first number. "That's the number of championships—Division *One* championships—that I have coached."

He circled the second number. "Thirty-seven. The number of kids I have coached who have gone on to full scholarships in college programs."

Next he circled the final number. "Two. The number of players I've coached who have gone on to play professional football." He paused. We hung on his next words. "One of them was up in the big leagues for just half a season, never was a starter. The other, I think you know. Jessie McCarthy."

"Of course we know him," Caleb said. "Everybody in the country knows him."

Jessie was a defensive lineman—like me—and was a star in the NFL.

"I was talking to Jessie yesterday and—"

"You were talking to him?" Robbie gasped.

Coach Barnes shrugged. "We talk all the time. He calls to ask advice or sometimes just to shoot the breeze. Anyway, he said he's going to drop in this summer to meet my new players."

"To meet us?" Caleb sounded like he couldn't believe his ears.

"And to maybe give some tips to our linemen. Jessie is living large, living the dream," Coach Barnes said. "A dream that everybody in this room has had at one time in their life. Is there anybody who hasn't thought about making it, going to college, being that one-in-a-million player who not only makes it to the NFL, but becomes a star? Well…anybody?"

Nobody answered. Who hadn't had that dream? Or the dream about hitting the homer that wins the World Series? Or playing in the NBA?

"Dreams do come true," Coach Barnes said, "but only for those who never sleep. If you snooze you lose. I'm now going to tell you boys—you men—my dream. Actually, it's my plan, because I always have a plan. Those who fail to plan, plan to fail. I want you all to remember those words—heck, I want you all to repeat them. Those who fail to plan…"

"Those who fail to plan," we all echoed.

"…plan to fail," Coach Barnes said.

"Plan to fail," we repeated.

"Say it again!" he ordered.

We repeated the words, this time louder and with more force and purpose.

"This is my plan," Coach Barnes said. "We're going to win the championship next year. The Division One championship."

"But we've always played Division Two," Caleb said.

"That was in the past. It's time to step up and play with the big boys—beat the big boys."

"We're not that big a school," somebody said. "Our student body isn't that big."

"I'm not interested in the size of the student body, but in the size of the heart inside the bodies on my team. Is there anybody here who doesn't think we can do it?"

Nobody answered.

"Because anybody who doesn't think we can win can walk through that door right now. As a matter of fact, I'll open the door myself and slam it behind them. Well, do you think we can do it? Yes or no?"

"We can do it," Caleb said.

"I heard the words, but I couldn't hear the attitude. Don't make it sound like a question or an apology. Make it sound like a statement."

"We can do it!" Caleb practically yelled. "We can do it!"

"What about the rest of you? What do you think?"

"We can do it!" everybody yelled.

"I know we can. If you can dream it, you can plan it, and if you can plan it, you can do it. We can do it. All of you, stand up."

We stumbled to our feet.

"Form a circle."

We all did what we were told.

"Now put out a hand—right here on top of mine."

We all extended our hands until there was a pile of hands on top of each other.

"I'm going to give you boys my word that I will do whatever, and I mean *whatever*, is necessary to help us reach our dream. Will you all do the same?"

We all nodded our heads and yelled out agreement. I felt a tingle go right up my spine. I felt as hyped as I had been during the big game—after the big game.

"It all begins right now, right here. On three, break. One, two, three."

"Break!" we all yelled out.

The bell suddenly rang, signaling the end of fourth period. It was lunch. As everybody stood around, talking and laughing, I walked over to the corner of the weight room. I sat down on the end of the bench and positioned myself under the bar. I started doing presses. One. Two. Three. Four. Five. I reached ten and put the bar back in place.

I looked around the room. The other guys were all at different pieces of equipment, working out. Coach Barnes was standing at my side.

"I figured I'd made the right choice for captain. Now I know."

I felt happy and excited—and a little bit guilty. Coach Reeves hadn't even cleaned out his office yet.

I owed him so much. He was the reason I had played in the first place, and then he'd worked with me to help me become a better player. He'd also been there when I was having trouble in math. He sat down and worked with me until I understood calculus. He didn't do that just so I could stay eligible to play ball. He just did it. I'd miss him. Still, this was pretty exciting.

Chapter Five

"What are you doing?" my mother asked as she padded into the kitchen in her slippers and pajamas.

"Eating," I mumbled through a big mouthful of cereal.

"You're always eating. What I meant is, what are you doing up at this hour? It's not even seven o'clock. You can't be starting work this early."

"The store doesn't even open until eight," I said. "I have a shift later on today. I'm working from noon to six."

I worked in the produce department of Dennis's No Frills Grocery Store. It was a nice job. I liked the people I worked with. Dennis was a great boss, and he always let me, and the other members of the team, change our shifts so we wouldn't miss games or practices.

"Then, getting back to my original question, why are you up?"

"I'm going to school."

"In case you hadn't noticed, it's summer vacation. You don't have to go to school," my mother said.

"I'm not taking a vacation this year. I'm going to school every day this summer to hit the weight room. You should see how amazing it is in there!"

They'd finished the weight room in record time, and it was everything that Coach Barnes had said it would be.

"I'm sure it's wonderful. What I don't understand is how come they don't have money for each student to have his own textbook, but they have money to spend on the football program."

"It was all donated," I explained.

"Maybe somebody should donate money for textbooks."

"I think that'll happen when everybody in town crowds into the stadium to watch people read their textbooks," I said.

"That won't happen in this town. Everybody is football crazy, maybe too much so," my mother said.

"That's not possible."

"Do you really think that you have to go in every day?" my mother asked.

"Gotta. I'm the captain and I have to set a good example."

My mother came over and gave me a kiss on the top of my head. "You always set a good example in everything. I'm so proud of you. I was proud of you long before you started playing football."

I felt embarrassed and happy. "I better get going."

"Why don't you wait and I'll drive you to school."

I shook my head. "That wouldn't work. I'm going to run to the school and get some work for my legs. Thanks, but no thanks. I gotta get going."

I stood up and cleared my place, putting the bowl and cup in the sink.

"I'll see you after work," I said.

"I'll make you something special for dinner," my mother said.

"If you want to make it really special, make it really big. I'm trying to bulk up."

"I'm glad to hear that. I was worried that you were wasting away," she joked.

"And do you think you could buy me some vitamins?" I asked.

"You've always hated vitamins," my mother said. "When you were little I even tried to get you to take those chewable ones, the ones shaped like little bears and bunnies."

"I was hoping that instead of bears and bunnies you could get me some vitamin C, and A and some E and—maybe you should just get me the whole alphabet."

"I'll get you whatever you want, but why this sudden interest in vitamins?" she asked.

"You can't run an engine without putting in the right fuel. That's what Coach Barnes said. I need vitamins to build up my strength."

"Your strength? You're as strong as an ox," she said.

"I want to be stronger than an ox. I only have fourteen weeks until our first game. That's fourteen weeks to make it happen."

That didn't seem like nearly enough time. I had no time to waste.

Chapter Six

I paused at the door to the weight room. The door was locked and there was a little touch pad to enter the code that would open it. It was a four-digit code—a very easy code to remember. One, one, one, one. Coach Barnes had told us that one was the only number we'd need to know because number two and up were for losers. I punched in the code and there was a loud click as the lock released. I pulled the door open. I expected that the lights would be off. Instead the hall was well lit and the door to the weight room was open. Had somebody gotten here before me? I heard the sound of weights being lifted. Who was it? Was it Caleb or Robbie or one of the other guys? Then again, it couldn't be Caleb. If he were here he'd be sitting on a bench, but not actually lifting any weights.

I poked my head through the door. There was a man—a big man—on a bench doing presses. He was focused on the bar he was pumping and didn't see me. He was grunting as he lifted, and his muscles—his big muscles—flexed. His arms were gigantic and his chest was as thick as a tree trunk. His head was shaved and shiny, and that made it harder to judge his age, but I figured he was in his twenties.

I did a quick count of the weight he was lifting, adding up the plates. There were over three hundred pounds on the bar! And he wasn't just lifting it—he was pumping it up and down, up and down, like his arms were pistons in a car. It looked like he wasn't even working that hard. How many had he done and how many was he going to do?

At that instant he lowered the bar into the cradle. He sat up, saw me and smiled. There were a couple of big, angry-looking zits on his face.

"Good morning. You have to be Michael," he said.

"Yeah, I am. How did you know?"

"Coach Barnes told me that he thought you'd be the first one here."

He stood up. I was surprised. He was really built, but he was short. I was a full head taller than he was. Somehow, when he was sitting on the bench, his muscles all big and bulging, I thought he was taller.

"I'm Tony," he said, offering me his hand. We shook. His grip was strong and powerful. "I'm the strength coach."

"We have a strength coach?"

"You do for the summer. I've been hired to create and monitor an individual program for every member of the team."

"You'll tell us what weights we should use?" I asked.

"What weights, what machines, how many reps, how often and in what order. But I'll be doing a lot more than that. I'll be looking at your diet, vitamins and food supplements."

"That's great. I was just telling my mother this morning that I needed some vitamins."

"You do, but tell her to save her money. We'll supply everything."

"Everything?" I asked in amazement.

"Everything except for the most important thing, and that you have to supply." He tapped me on the chest. "The heart. You supply the heart and we'll supply the rest. So what do you weigh? Around 225 would be my guess."

"I was 229 on my scale when I weighed myself this morning."

"Forget your scale. Those bathroom jobs are never very accurate. You'll get weighed every day here. Turn around."

"What?"

"Turn around. I want to have a look at you."

Slowly, feeling very self-conscious, I turned.

"Thick chest, good-size arms, pecs are big, your legs look a little flabby."

I felt uneasy, like I was a prize horse.

"How much can you bench press?" he asked.

"I can do 210 pounds," I said proudly— that was more than anybody else on the team, including the seniors who had graduated.

"Oh, don't worry about that. We'll have you pushing some real weight soon enough."

My jaw practically dropped open. What did he mean by that?

"If you follow your program, you'll be hoisting closer to three within twelve weeks."

"Three? Like in three hundred pounds?"

"That's a minimum goal for somebody who's going to weigh in at 260 pounds."

"But I only weigh 229."

"You only weigh 229 now. Twelve weeks from now is a whole different game. You don't do a lot of weights, do you?" Tony asked.

"I was in here a lot last year," I said, shaking my head. "A couple of times a week."

"A couple of times? I thought you said a lot. Twice a week isn't going to cut it, and you probably had nobody to train you. Most likely it was a bunch of you boys in here, more pretending and playing than actually working. We'll take care of that. You have a good platform to build on. You're naturally a big guy. How big is your dad?"

"He's big," I said. Actually, I remembered him as being huge, but most men are pretty big compared to nine-year-olds. It had been almost eight years since I'd seen him.

"How much does he weigh and how tall is he?"

"A couple of inches taller than me and more weight," I said. I wasn't sure of his exact height or weight, but I didn't like to talk about that.

"That's great. It means we have room for growth. Have you ever taken megadoses of vitamins or used food supplements?"

"Some chewable vitamins when I was small."

"That isn't quite what I was talking about. What that means is that most of the things

we're going to try, you've never tried. Forget the 300 pounds. We might get you up to
bench pressing 325 pounds. They call you
The Moose, right?"

I nodded.

"By the time I'm through with you, they'll
be calling you a herd of moose."

"That would be great."

"All you have to do is follow the program
and work hard."

"I'll work hard," I said.

"I believe you. You know who you remind
me of? Your attitude?"

"Who?"

"Jessie McCarthy."

"I remind you of Jessie McCarthy?" I said,
shocked.

"Yep. Kid always had the right attitude. I
started training him when he was about your
age. Helped him to become everything he is
today. He still comes back to me. He's got
all those fancy trainers and therapists and
coaches up there in the NFL, but it's still me
he calls when he needs to talk."

"That's incredible."

"So, I think it's time we got down to work."

"You got it," I said. "I'll do whatever you want, whatever it takes."

"That's the attitude I like. We'll talk about your individual program and then get you started. There's no time to lose."

Chapter Seven

"Excuse me, young man, do you have any bananas?" came a voice from behind me.

I took a deep breath before turning around. I was standing in front of a mountain of bananas, and beside me was a cart filled with even more bananas that I was going to put on the top of the mountain.

"Yes, ma'am, we have bananas and—," I turned around. It was my mother, standing there with a big goofy smile on her face.

"Mom!"

She started giggling. I always came home and told her about the stupid questions I was asked by customers.

"What are you doing here?" I asked.

She pointed at the cart at her side. It was practically overflowing with groceries. "I thought I could shop and then offer you a drive home after your shift is over."

"That would be great. My legs are really sore and tired."

"You must have moved a lot of bananas today," she said.

"I did. I moved ninety-six boxes, which is 9,600 individual bananas. But that's not what got me so tired. Tony had me working my lower body."

"Tony?" she said.

"He's our team's strength coach."

"Your team has a strength coach?" she asked in disbelief.

"Yeah, isn't that incredible?"

"It's something," she said.

"He's only here for the summer. Normally he just works with the pros. Do you know he's Jessie McCarthy's personal trainer?"

"Who's she?" Mom asked.

"She? Jessie McCarthy isn't a girl. He's a professional foot—"

She started laughing again and I knew she'd just been putting me on. "I know who he is," she said. "So why would this Tony come here to work with some high school kids lifting weights?"

"Coach Barnes arranged it. He can arrange anything. Besides, it's not just weight training. He's working out an individual training plan for us that includes diet and food supplements and—that reminds me, you don't have to buy vitamins. They provide it all."

"That's good. Now if I could just get them to pay for your groceries," my mother said. "By the way, guess who dropped into the bank today."

I knew in my head it could have been any of dozens of people, but my heart gave another answer—my dad. He hadn't lived with us for almost nine years, and I hadn't even seen him for eight, but that thought still popped into my head. Sometimes I thought I saw him on street corners or in stores as we passed by.

I remembered the night he left. The yelling and screaming and crying. The holes in the wall that he'd made with his fists—holes that weren't fixed for a year after that. I thought my mother left them there to remind her.

The yelling and the tears weren't uncommon. None of it was. That time, though, he left and didn't come back. He still came around and saw me a couple of times a week and took me out. Then he moved out of town. There were letters and phone calls at first and then nothing. Nothing for the last seven years.

My father loved football. He played for his high school. When I was playing I sometimes pretended that he was up in the stands watching. Who knows, maybe he was. The crowds were pretty big. More likely he wasn't there, but that didn't mean he couldn't have read about what I was doing. Maybe he'd read that our team won the championship and that I was the MVP.

"That Coach Barnes of yours came into the bank today," my mother said.

"What was he doing there?"

"He was opening an account, but it looked like he was running for mayor the way he was shaking hands and greeting people."

"He's pretty good with people. Did you talk to him?"

"He made a point of coming over to talk to me. He certainly has a lot of teeth, and they're very white, unnaturally white."

"What did you talk about?" I asked.

"You and football."

"What did he have to say?"

"He had nothing but good things to say. He certainly knows a great deal about you and our lives."

"He knows a lot about everything. He's an amazing coach."

"Funny, he reminded me more of a used car salesman." She paused. "Or maybe he should be writing greeting cards or bumper stickers or those little messages you get in fortune cookies."

"I don't follow," I said.

"He just seems to talk in tiny bursts of words, all those little sayings of his."

"He just likes to say things that are inspirational," I said, defending him.

"It was like he was trying to sell me something."

"He is selling something," I said. "He's selling confidence, a winning attitude, a positive way of—"

"Excuse me."

I turned around. It was a woman standing beside her grocery cart.

"Can you tell me the price of bananas?" she asked.

Right above my head, in numbers as big as my head, was the price.

I pointed at the sign. "Sixty-nine cents a pound, ma'am."

"Oh, I didn't notice." She grabbed a big bunch, put them in her cart and walked away.

My mother was covering her mouth to keep from laughing.

"You see," I said. "I get the stupidest questions."

"There are no stupid questions," my mother said.

"Okay, that was a smart question asked by a stupid person."

"You handled it well. Very diplomatic, very polite. I guess that's why you're the employee of the month again. I saw your smiling face at the front."

A big picture of the employee of the month was posted by the front door.

"Why didn't you tell me?" she asked.

"It's no big deal. I think they gave it to me because I recovered that fumble."

"I think they gave it to you because you're a good, hardworking, polite employee. Now, can you tell me where the green peppers are?"

"Mom," I said, shaking my head.

"No, seriously, I don't know."

"Oh. Far wall. In the corner. You can get the good ones by digging into the back. And if you want to know the price, it'll be on a big sign right above them."

She smiled. I loved making her smile. "I'll see you right after work. Maybe we'll stop on the way home and pick up supper—your choice."

"You're the best," I said.

She flashed that smile again and I watched her walk away. She really was the best.

chapter Eight

I strained under the weight, the bar balancing on my shoulders, behind my neck. In the last two weeks I'd increased my squats by twenty-five pounds. Part of the reason for the gain was that I'd learned how to balance the bar better. The other part was that I was stronger. I could feel it in my legs and see it in the mirror. Maybe I hated squats, but I'd keep on doing them. And I was sure that in eight weeks I'd hate them more often and with more weight.

I finished the last squat and carefully lowered the bar into the cradle with a metallic thud.

All around me, working the different machines, were the members of the team—our returning players from last year and a half-dozen others, students who Coach Barnes thought had potential and could make the team.

On the far wall were painted the words "Wall of Fame." All the guys called it the Wall of Pain. There, for everybody to see, were our individual plans and results. In neat rows and columns were our weekly goals, each week listed separately until the first week of September.

Success or failure was there for everybody to see. So far, all we'd had were successes. Each guy, each week, had met or beat his goals. With Tony's help and Coach's encouragement, we seemed unstoppable.

There were also words of wisdom painted on the other walls: *No Pain, No Gain; Reach for the Stars; You miss every shot you don't take*. When I read those words I could hear

Coach's voice. Maybe he did talk like he was writing bumper stickers, but they were sayings that did inspire me. He was one smart guy.

I walked over to where Caleb was working. He was skipping—one of the best ways to improve foot speed and strength. For the receivers, bulking up was the opposite of what they wanted to do. They had to build speed and agility and vertical leap, not raw strength.

Caleb was whipping the rope around, doing double skips and crossovers, the sound of the rope whistling as he worked. The rope sped up, faster and faster, and then he did a triple pass and stopped.

"Need...a...drink," Caleb panted, sweat pouring down his face.

That sounded like a good idea. We walked over to the big fridge in the corner. It was filled with power drinks and protein shakes.

"What do you want?" I asked as I opened the door.

"Shake. Love those shakes."

I grabbed two and handed one to him. Caleb flipped off the plastic top and took a big sip.

"I've been bugging Tony to tell me what's in these so I can make my own at home," Caleb said.

Tony made up the protein shakes, and he wouldn't tell anybody what was in them. Some of the ingredients were obvious: ice cream, milk, protein powder and vitamins. But exactly what and the amounts were like a state secret.

"I just know that whatever it is, they work," I said as I slurped down my shake as well.

Tony was at the far side of the room, working with one of the guys. He was always working with somebody or working out himself.

"Tony's a good guy," Caleb said. "Shame he doesn't have a life."

"I was thinking the same thing. He's here all the time."

"Doesn't he have a wife or girlfriend or something?" Caleb asked.

"I think this is his life."

"Then again, with those skin problems maybe getting a girlfriend isn't that easy," Caleb said.

It wasn't just his face, but his arms and back were covered with acne—big, ugly-looking zits.

"Yeah, it's—"

The phone in Tony's office started ringing. I yelled out for him, but between the music and the distance he couldn't hear me.

"I'll get the phone and you get Tony," I said to Caleb.

The office door was open. I grabbed the ringing phone.

"Hello," I said as I picked it up.

"Good morning. This isn't Tony. Who is this?"

"No, sir, Coach Barnes," I said. I'd recognized his voice. "This is Michael."

"So, Moose, are you adding secretary to your role as team captain?" he asked.

"If that's what it takes to win, I will."

He laughed. "That's the attitude, and as we both know, attitude leads to altitude. The better the attitude, the higher you'll fly."

"Yes, sir. Do you want me to get Tony?"

"If you could just tell him that I'll be a little late today. I have a meeting down at the Rotary Club at noon. I'm going to try to convince them to put up funds to replace our tackling sled."

"That would be great!" The old one was pretty beaten up.

"Only the best for the best," he said. "Tell him I'll be in around 1:00. Are you going to be there still?"

"If you want me to, I will."

"I want you to. See you then. And Moose, I'm real proud of the way you're leading by example. A coach couldn't ask for a better captain."

"Thank you, sir. See you at one o'clock."

Chapter Nine

Coach closed the door, and the sound of the music playing in the weight room was muffled. He settled into the chair behind Tony's desk. I took a seat across from him.

"You're working really hard," Coach Barnes said.

"Thanks. I'm trying my best."

"Actually, everybody out there is trying his best," he said, pointing out through the closed door. "Unfortunately, doing their best might not be good enough."

I was confused. What did that mean?

"What I'm going to tell you has to stay between me and you. You can't talk to the other players about this."

"I won't, not if you don't want me to. You can trust me, sir."

"I know I can, Moose." He got up from his chair, circled around and sat on the edge of the desk, right in front of me.

"These are really good boys. They're all working hard. What I don't know, though, is, do they have enough to win?"

I was shocked. I'd never heard him talk about anything but success.

"I'm going to have more than a few boys on this squad who are going to be starters but really shouldn't be. I just don't have anybody better."

"You tell them what they need to do and they'll do it," I said.

"It's not that easy. They'd have to grow four inches, gain fifty pounds and become more coordinated. There's only so much they can do. What we need is for those who have the ability—people like you—to make up for what they can't do." He paused. "I need you to be even better."

"You know I'll do whatever needs to be done," I said.

"Injuries are going to be critical for us. We don't have any depth. Do you think people would be willing to play through pain?"

"No pain, no gain," I said, echoing his words. "We'll do what has to be done."

"You can't speak for everybody. I'm asking you. Would you play through the pain of an injury?"

"I'd do whatever it takes."

"Whatever?" he asked.

"Anything."

Coach didn't say anything for a while. He just sat there, staring down at the desk. Didn't he believe me? Finally he spoke.

"You know those protein shakes that you all drink," he said. "Do you know what's in them?"

"Tony's secret recipe. Lots of ice cream

and milk, but he won't tell anybody all of the ingredients."

"He won't even tell me, but I know that all of them are bought in nutrition stores, all of them are over-the-counter ingredients. Legal ingredients."

Legal? I was reassured but disturbed at the same time. I hadn't even thought that anything in those drinks could be illegal.

"Some of those ingredients are anabolic— that means building muscle tissue. That's why you and your teammates are getting stronger so fast. I guess you've noticed."

"It would be hard not to notice," I said. I looked down at my arm. It was bigger.

"I'm going to be honest with you, Moose. I need you to be a leader both off the field and on it. I need you to make up for the limitations of your teammates. When you're on that field, I need you to be unstoppable. I need you to be a one-man wrecking squad. I need you to be a monster out there. Championships are won on defense, and you need to be the heart of that defense. Can you do that?"

I felt my heart racing. "I'll try."

"I need you to do more than try."

"I'll do it."

"Will you? Will you do whatever it takes?"

"Anything."

He smiled. "You know, my sons are just little guys. I hope that they can grow up to be as fine a young man as you've become."

I felt myself blushing.

"I'm as proud of you as if you were my own." He paused. "There's still one more step you could take."

"What is it?" My mind raced, trying to think of what it could be. Did he want me here more often, working out? What could it be?

He put a hand on my shoulder. "I want you to talk to Tony."

Chapter Ten

Within fifteen minutes of me talking to Coach Barnes, Tony came up and told me that the two of us should talk—but that that talk would have to be done later on, privately.

Maybe I wasn't the quickest person in the world, but as I spent the rest of that day thinking, I was pretty sure I knew what we were going to be talking about—steroids. It was the only thing that made sense. What else could make me stronger? What else would he want Tony to talk to me about—especially in private?

We'd learned about steroids in health class. They could help you build bigger muscles and get stronger, but they had side effects. Things like bad skin and baldness—was Tony bald? The way his head was shaved and shiny, who could tell? I also knew there were long-term effects of steroids. Couldn't they cause kidney problems? Or was it cancer? I should have paid more attention. I could still look it up, but not now. Maybe he was going to talk about something else. Maybe.

A car's horn startled me out of my thoughts. It was a big black SUV, and as I watched, the darkly tinted driver's window glided down. It was Tony.

"Get in!" he yelled.

I climbed in.

"Nice wheels," I said as I settled into my seat.

"Thanks. You want to drive?"

"Me? I don't have a driver's license."

"Do you want to drive anyway?"

"I think it would be better if I didn't."

"Suit yourself, but sometimes you have to push those boundaries a bit."

We started driving. It was strange seeing him someplace other than the weight room. It was almost like he'd been living there, sleeping on the exercise mats. We drove along in silence, music playing softly in the background.

"Did Coach tell you what we're going to talk about?" Tony asked.

"A way to get stronger."

"Did he tell you what that would involve?"

I shook my head. "But I think I have an idea."

"Go on," he said.

Now I felt like I shouldn't talk. What if I was wrong? "Maybe I shouldn't say it."

"Maybe you should."

I swallowed hard. "Steroids," I said. My voice was barely loud enough to be heard over the CD.

"And what do you think about them?" he asked.

"I don't know exactly what to think."

"You know that I take them," Tony said.

"I thought that maybe you might have," I admitted.

"Nobody gets this big and strong without them. Have you heard about the health issues?"

"Some."

"What have you heard?" Tony asked.

"They can cause baldness, kidney problems, cancer and skin problems."

"Just for the record, my skin was bad before I took steroids, and I shave my head because the babes love their men to be bald and built." He paused. "You must find the babes go after you, right?" he said. He laughed and reached over and gave me a little tap on the arm.

"And all that other stuff, cancer, kidney problems. Do you know where all those results came from?"

I shook my head.

"Studies on rats. They gave them gigantic doses and kept giving it to them until they croaked. Most of those studies are just garbage. I know lots and lots of people who are on the juice, and none of them have any problems."

That was encouraging to hear.

"Besides, nobody's talking about you doing anything long-term. A twelve-week cycle. Maybe a second twelve-week cycle in the spring in the playoffs when the college scouts are all there. That's all. Do you think Coach Barnes would ever recommend anything that would hurt you?" Tony asked. "You should hear the way he talks about you—like a son—like he still talks about Jessie."

"Jessie McCarthy?"

"Coach says he's the best captain he's ever had, but he said that might change."

"Wow," I said softly. "Could I ask you a question?"

"Shoot?"

"Jessie...did he? Does he do..."

"Won't answer that question. Could if I wanted to, but I won't. Just like I'd never answer that question about you. What happens between you and me stays here. It's nobody's business but ours."

"But isn't using steroids sort of like cheating?" I asked.

"It would be if you were the only one doing it. Half the kids on the line who are standing across from you, trying to block you, are on the juice. We're just trying to give you what you need to even up the score."

I nodded in agreement. I couldn't afford to let anybody else have that advantage.

"Is it just me or other people on the team?" I asked.

"Right now it's just you. Maybe later we'll let a few more in. But you can't talk to anybody, even your teammates, about it, and they won't talk to you about it either. I'm the only one anybody will talk to. It won't be many, just those that have a shot."

"A shot at what?" I asked.

"Scholarships, college ball, maybe even the whole thing—professional ball," Tony said.

"You think I could play pro ball?" I gasped.

"You have the best shot of anybody on this team. But first things first. I figure you're a lock for college. We'll be spending time trying to figure out your best offer and which school you want to go to. That can be confusing, but Coach can help make that right, so don't worry. You do want to go to college, right?"

"Yeah, sure, of course."

"It's just you and your mother, right?" Tony asked.

"Yeah."

"And she works in a bank as a teller?"

"She's the head teller," I said.

"That's great—you must be proud of her. But even head tellers can't make that much money, and college is expensive. I think you might just get a full ride."

"A full ride?"

"All expenses paid. Your mother won't have to put up a cent for you to go to college."

"That would be unbelievable!"

"That's where you're wrong," Tony said. "It's all believable, all doable, all possible." He paused. "Well?"

I didn't answer right away.

"It's not just for you," Tony said. "It's for your teammates, for Coach, for your future, for your mother. If you started and wanted to stop, then you just stop, okay?"

I still didn't answer. What was I supposed to say?

"Well?"

Slowly I nodded my head. "I'll do it."

He smiled broadly. "You won't regret it!" he exclaimed.

I hoped he was right.

"I'll arrange everything. We'll start tomorrow. And what we talked about is between you and me. Don't even talk to Coach about it except through me. Oh, and one more thing. We never use the word steroid again. It's just juice. Special juice. Okay?"

Again I nodded. I felt like I was already questioning my decision, but how could I say no with all of those people depending on me, with my future depending on it? I had no choice but to try.

Chapter Eleven

I closed the door of the bathroom stall and pulled out the pills. Nine of them. Six white and three orange. I rolled them around in my hand. How could these little pills make such a difference? I didn't know exactly how they worked, but I knew they did. The results were clear to be seen. In only four weeks I was pressing and lifting and moving more weight than I'd ever been able to do in my entire life.

I put all nine pills in my mouth, took a sip of water and swallowed them down. I didn't like pills, but it was getting easier. That was good because the number of pills I was going to take was going to increase for another two weeks. It was called pyramiding. It involved starting with a low dose and building it up slowly for six weeks and then decreasing it every week for another six weeks until I stopped completely. Twelve weeks. That was the cycle. That wasn't that much.

I was also taking three different types of steroids—I was stacking them. Stacking was supposed to be more effective than just using one type.

I left the stall and went out to wash my hands. I stood there and looked at myself in the mirror. I flexed my biceps. I couldn't help but smile at my reflection. I was definitely bigger and more defined. That wasn't just my imagination. It was in black and white, right up there on the Wall of Fame.

Almost as obvious was the red zit on my forehead. It looked like I was growing a horn. I had a couple of smaller ones on my neck, and one big one on my back. But I'd had pimples before. That didn't mean it was a side effect of the juice. And even if it was, so what? I'd trade a couple of pimples for this extra power and potential.

I left the washroom and returned to the weight room. It was a buzz of activity. People were lifting, skipping, running on the treadmill. The TVs were all on—three different shows—none of them audible over the pounding beat of the sound system.

Caleb was sitting on the universal gym, resting between sets.

"You going home soon?" I asked over the music.

"Soon. You?"

"Leaving, but not going home. I have a shift at—" I stopped and spun around in reaction to some yelling. Two of the guys were exchanging angry words. Then one reached out and gave the other a push, and the first pushed back.

"Come on," I said to Caleb. We ran over to get in between them. Out of nowhere, Tony rushed over and grabbed me by the arm.

"Leave 'em alone," Tony said.

"What?"

"Leave 'em alone. Can't be a pussycat in the weight room and a tiger on the field."

"But—"

"Don't worry. I won't let it get out of hand."

The two guys kept pushing and yelling, and I was positive they were going to come to blows. Then they both turned and walked away.

"Not much of a fight," Tony said.

"You sound disappointed," Caleb said.

Tony shrugged and walked away.

"What was that all about?" Caleb asked.

"I don't know what they were fighting about."

"I don't mean the fight. I mean Tony," he said.

"He just wanted to let them work it out," I said.

"Work it out or duke it out? If you ask me, he wanted them to come to blows."

"He would have stopped them if that happened."

"Before or after somebody got hurt?"

"Tony would have taken care of it," I argued.

Caleb shook his head. "You got an awful lot of faith in that guy. Can we talk?"

"What do you think we're doing?"

"Not here." Caleb turned and walked away. I followed him out of the weight room, down the hall and out into the courtyard. It was hot and the sun was shining brightly. I used my hand to shield my eyes.

"Look," Caleb began, "I know something's going on here. I'm not stupid. Those special shakes that Tony makes—do you know what's in them?"

"Nobody knows that but Tony."

"Well I think I know. I think there's something that's not legal. I think we're being fed steroids."

A chill went up my spine.

"Tony told me that there's nothing illegal in those drinks," I said. "Just stuff he gets at health food stores."

"There's lots of stuff that's sold legally that is still illegal to take in sports. They test for lots of stuff in the Olympics, on pro teams. Look, everybody's getting too strong too fast. Something's not right. Besides, haven't you seen how people are acting, like those two inside just now? Everybody seems to be on edge, picking fights with each other. I'm edgy. For the first time in my life I'm having trouble sleeping at night. It's like I can't turn off my head."

I'd been having trouble sleeping too, but I wasn't going to admit it. Not now.

"Maybe there's just a lot on your mind," I suggested.

"There is a lot on my mind. I'm wondering if we're being doped without knowing it."

"It's not like that. If they wanted you to use steroids, Tony would ask you," I said.

"How can you be so—?" Caleb stopped. He looked dead serious. "You know that because they asked you, didn't they? Moose, you gotta be honest with me. Are you using steroids?"

I didn't answer. I had been feeling guilty already for not talking to Caleb. I knew he wasn't going to be taking them—receivers didn't need to bulk up.

"Well?" he asked.

"I'm not doing anything wrong," I finally said. "I'm just trying to do what's best for everybody. For the team, for my mother, for my future. That's all. You don't have to worry."

"I don't have to worry, but I'm going to anyway," Caleb said. "And you should be worried too."

chapter Twelve

I slammed the door with such force that the glass rattled. For a split second I thought it was going to break.

"Michael?" my mother called out as she rushed into the hall. "What was that noise?"

"Nothing. I closed the door."

"What are you doing here?" she asked.

"I live here!" I snapped.

"I mean what are you doing here now? Aren't you supposed to be working?"

"Supposed to be."

"Then why aren't you?" she asked.

"I don't want to talk about it," I said as I brushed past her and headed for the kitchen.

"I need you to talk about it," she said as she trailed in behind me. "Did something happen?"

I flung open the fridge door and grabbed a Coke. "I'm going to my room."

She stood in the doorway, blocking my way. "You're not going anywhere until I get an answer."

"Look, it's no big deal. It happens to people all the time," I said. "I was suspended for the day."

"Suspended! What happened?"

"Nothing."

"Something had to happen."

I was angry and embarrassed. I really didn't want to talk about it.

"Please. Tell me," she said.

"There was this woman…"

"What woman?"

"At the store. I don't know who she was. I was moving some empty boxes…"

"Yeah, go on."

"And she cut me off with her grocery cart and the boxes tumbled over and one of them bounced against the side of her cart," I said.

"Accidents happen," my mother said.

"That's what I said. And it wasn't like anybody got hurt."

"That's the important part."

"You'd think that, wouldn't you!" I snapped. "But she just starts yelling at me, and screaming like I'd tried to kill her!"

"That's awful."

"Everybody's staring at me, and she keeps on screaming, getting louder and louder… and then…I told her to shut up, and she wouldn't. So I started yelling at her, telling her what a stupid witch she was and—"

"Michael, you didn't," my mother said.

"She deserved it, the stupid—the stupid—woman." I felt my temper rising as I talked about her. "I had to fight the urge to reach out and give her a smack!"

"Michael, don't even joke about that."

"Who's joking? I had to stop myself from giving her a backhand across the—"

I was stopped by the expression on my mother's face. She looked shocked. No, worse, disappointed.

"I didn't hit her," I protested.

My mother looked like she was going to burst into tears. Suddenly she turned around and ran up the stairs. I started after her and then stopped. What had I done?

I spun around and, without realizing what I was doing, smashed my fist against the wall. The plaster exploded and my hand disappeared into the wall! I pulled my hand out and punched the wall again and again and again, until it was pocked with holes, the powder from the plaster floating through the air.

I slumped to the ground. My hand was sore and the knuckles were cut. I could see it starting to swell up.

What had I done? My stomach heaved violently and I thought I was going to throw up. I stumbled to my feet. My legs were all rubbery and I staggered toward the bathroom. I pushed open the door and dropped down to my knees in front of the toilet. I started to vomit long and hard.

As my stomach settled, my head began to spin. How could I have yelled at that woman like that? It was like I was insane—the look on my mother's face, the holes in the wall— holes like my father had made that last night before he left. This was all so unbelievable. How could I have done any of this? There was only one answer. It had to be the juice. I'd read about it. Mood swings and anger problems, like those guys fighting today. Roid rage.

I crawled across the floor and opened the cupboard under the sink. I dug into the back. There in the far corner, hidden inside an old gym bag, was my stash. I pulled out the bottle. It contained the rest of the steroids for the next eight weeks. I opened the top. I had to get rid of them. I held the open bottle over the toilet. All I had to do was dump them and they'd be gone. That's all I had to do.

I sat there on the cold floor, the bottle balanced in my hand, thinking of what it would mean. Who would I disappoint if I flushed them away? Who would I disappoint if I didn't? I just sat there, thinking. I didn't have an answer.

Chapter Thirteen

I was startled out of my sleep by a ringing phone. I rolled off the sofa and onto my feet. I'd fallen asleep watching TV. The TV was off. That meant my mother had turned it off. She must have seen the holes in the wall. She knew what I'd done. I felt so ashamed. That was why I hadn't wanted to see her or talk to her. What was I going to say to her?

The phone kept ringing. I ran to pick it up.

"Hello," I said.

"Hey, Moose, you just get up?" It was Caleb.

"Just this second."

"That's what I figured because you didn't answer the first few times you were called."

"You called me earlier?"

"Me and Mrs. Perkins. When she couldn't get you, she asked if I'd keep trying."

"Mrs. Perkins called me?"

"She called everybody on the team."

"Why would she be calling people? Isn't she off for the summer?" Mrs. Perkins was the school secretary.

"She was calling to set up a meeting. She said Coach wanted everybody to meet in the weight room at ten."

"Why would there be a meeting?"

"She didn't tell and I didn't ask. You got just enough time to get yourself ready and get there."

"What do you think it's about?" I asked.

"Probably wants to tell us some more little sayings and make us work harder. Maybe hand out some steroids."

"Don't joke about that," I said.

"Who's joking? You okay?"

"I'm fine!" I snapped and then instantly regretted my angry tone. He was just worried about me. Heck, I was worried about me. Maybe I should tell Caleb what was happening.

"So I'll see you there," Caleb said.

"Sure. Thanks for calling."

I put the phone down. I didn't know what this meeting was about, but I felt uneasy, more than uneasy. I looked at my hand. It was swollen and painful to the touch. What an idiot I was!

The pills were back in my gym bag. I hadn't dumped them, but I wasn't sure if I was going to take them anymore. Maybe I could just pretend to take them and not tell anybody. No, that wouldn't work. Tony would be able to tell by the results. No matter how hard I worked over the next eight weeks, I couldn't get the same results. There didn't seem to be an answer—at least no answer that didn't involve disappointing somebody, letting somebody down.

I walked down the hall. I tried to look away, but I couldn't avoid seeing the holes. I was going to go straight from the meeting to the hardware store. I was going to buy a piece of drywall and some plaster and paint. I couldn't change what I'd done, but I could have it all fixed before my mother got home from work that night. Then I'd apologize and promise not to ever let something like that happen again. Could I keep that promise?

I was going to ask Caleb to help me fix the wall. He was good with that sort of stuff. That was one of the decisions I'd made. The other was that I was going to talk to him. I'd make him promise not to tell anybody and to let me make my own decision, but to help me with that decision. I could trust him. Actually, there was nobody else I could trust with this.

I bumped into a couple of other guys on the way into the school. They were laughing and joking around. Nobody else seemed worried. Maybe there was nothing to worry about. Maybe being paranoid was just another symptom of steroid use.

I hadn't taken any this morning. Missing one part of the day wouldn't make any difference, but would it hurt me?

It was a few minutes before ten, and almost everybody was assembled in the weight room. Caleb came over and sat down beside me.

It was strange being here without loud music pumping through the room or anybody sweating away on the weights. Looking up, I noticed the Wall of Fame and all of the progress charts were gone. Why weren't they there?

All that was left were the inspirational quotes. I looked at them, from quote to quote. My eyes stopped on one: *Show me a good loser and I'll show you a loser*. That one was positioned on the wall so that I stared right at it when I was doing my squats. I still hated squats and I'd learned to hate that quote. What was wrong with being a good loser? Wasn't that better than being a bad winner?

"I wonder where Tony is," Caleb said.

"Maybe he's in his office."

Caleb shook his head. "His SUV isn't in the lot. I don't think he's here."

"Probably coming with Coach Barnes."

I looked over at the clock. It was exactly 10:00, and Coach Barnes was a stickler for being on time.

Almost on cue, the office door opened. It was Coach Reeves! What was he doing here? I jumped up from my chair, as did everybody else, and we rushed over to him.

"I'm thrilled to see you all again too!" Coach Reeves responded. "But I need you all to sit down. We have to talk."

We settled back into our seats. If I was anxious before, I was really anxious now.

There was a rattling sound and I realized where it was coming from. Coach was shaking a can of spray paint. He walked over to the wall and started painting. He was spraying over all the sayings that lined the walls. Gone was *No Pain, No Gain*; gone was *Reach for the Stars*. He painted over the last half of *Show me a good loser and I'll show you a loser*, so that it only read *Show me a good loser*. He sprayed over the last part of *Winning isn't everything, it's the only thing!* Now it read *Winning isn't everything*. Finally he sprayed over the word *Fame* and in its place crudely painted *Shame*, so it was now the Wall of Shame.

We all sat there in stunned silence, watching him work. This was crazy. Finished, he dropped the can to the floor with a metallic thud.

"Thank you all for coming to my meeting," Coach Reeves said.

"We're glad to be here," Caleb said, "but we didn't know it was your meeting. Mrs. Perkins just said we were to meet with our coach."

"You are meeting with your coach. Your old, or, I guess, newest coach."

"You're our coach again?" I gasped.

"Are you disappointed, Michael?" Coach Reeves asked.

"No! Never! Of course not! I just don't understand."

"That's what I'm going to explain. They asked me to come out of retirement for one more year, and I agreed. Coach Barnes is gone. His assistant, Tony, is gone."

"Gone where?" Robbie asked.

Coach shook his head. "That will be determined by the courts."

"Courts?"

"The chief of police called last night. He wanted the school to know—for you all to know—before the press conference. Yesterday, as part of a large-scale police operation, Jessie McCarthy, along with a number of other professional football players, was arrested and charged with the illegal possession, use and sale of steroids."

"I saw that on the late news last night," Robbie said, and a couple of the other guys nodded in agreement. I hadn't seen or heard anything.

"What hasn't been announced yet is that, as part of the investigation, Mr. McCarthy revealed his source of illegal drugs."

I knew what he was going to say.

"The man who has been working as your strength coach, Tony, was subsequently arrested for trafficking in steroids. A search of his apartment, and this office," Coach Reeves said, gesturing over his shoulder, "revealed massive quantities of steroids."

I glanced around the room. Lots of the guys had their eyes on the floor. People looked uncomfortable, upset, scared. Nobody looked surprised.

"Tony then revealed that he was not operating alone. Coach Barnes was part of the steroid ring, and this included selling and distributing steroids to high school students. This has been confirmed at his old school." He paused and looked around. "And I hate to think it, but I suspect it also took place here as well."

Nobody answered.

"I want to apologize to all of you," Coach Reeves said.

"You want to apologize to us?" Caleb asked.

"Yes, this mess is all my fault. I should have known better. My instincts told me this was wrong. Why would he want to come to this school? To this town?"

"He wanted us to become champions," somebody said.

"He wanted you to be his ticket to a college coaching position or even the pros. He thought that if he could take a Division

Two school and make it the Division One champion, that everybody would notice and he'd be on his way. The problem was that he didn't care what, or who, got in his way or who he had to hurt to get there."

He looked back at the wall. "Winning isn't everything. There's nothing wrong with being a good loser. It's better to lose fairly than to win by cheating."

What was going to happen now? What was going to happen to me?

"You're all going to be interviewed by the police," Coach Reeves said.

My heart rose up into my throat.

"What should we tell them?" Caleb asked.

"You should tell them the truth. The sign of a winner isn't that he doesn't make mistakes, but that he owns up to those mistakes." He paused. "Doesn't anybody have any questions?"

"And if somebody did use steroids?" Caleb asked. I knew he was asking that question for me.

"I've been assured that if they tell the truth, no charges will be laid against them, and we'll be here—I'll be here—to help make things right."

Everybody sat silently. I knew it couldn't be just me—could it? It didn't matter. Slowly I got to my feet.

"I'll talk to them," I said. "I'll tell them whatever they need to know."

Robbie got to his feet. "I'll talk to them too. I'll tell them the truth."

Another guy stood up, then a fourth and a fifth and a sixth, until eleven of us were standing.

"I want you to know—all of you—how proud I am. This was the first step, and that's often the hardest step, toward us putting things back in order. I want you all to go home now."

Slowly, silently, everybody shuffled toward the door.

"Michael, could I have a word with you?" Coach Reeves asked.

I moved off to the side and waited until the last guy had left. I felt so awful. I'd let him down. He must be so disappointed in me.

"This is going to be a tough year," Coach

Reeves said. "Thank goodness I have a good captain to help me make this work."

"After what I did, you still want me to be the captain?" I asked in amazement.

"Now more than ever. You made a mistake and you probably did it because you wanted to help the team, to lead them to victory."

I nodded my head.

"Coach Barnes was pretty slick. Slick enough to fool me, so why not you too?"

"It was Tony who convinced me."

"The words may have come out of Tony's mouth, but they belonged to Coach Barnes. He used those words to seduce you with your own dreams. And do you know the scariest part?"

I shook my head.

"He's not alone. There are people like him everywhere. They're not coaches, they're drug pushers. They spend their time convincing kids, even middle school kids, that they need these drugs to compete or win or get to the next level. People have to stand up to them."

"But...but...I didn't."

"Yes you did. You did it today." He put a hand on my shoulder. "When you stood up right here, right now, you were showing leadership. Everybody makes mistakes. We're going to need a good leader to make things right." He paused. "I don't know how we'll do this season, whether we'll win it all or lose every single game. What I do know is that no matter what the score is, we'll walk off the field with our heads held high. We'll walk away knowing that we played the game fair and square and to the best of our ability. Do you know what that makes us?"

I shook my head.

"Winners."

OTHER TITLES IN THE
ORCA SOUNDINGS SERIES

Also by Eric Walters

Overdrive

"Go! Get out of here!"

I saw red flashing lights behind me in the distance. For a split second I took my foot off the accelerator. Then I pressed down harder and took a quick left turn.

Jake has finally got his driver's license, and tonight he has his brother's car as well. He and his friend Mickey take the car out and cruise the strip. When they challenge another driver to a road race, a disastrous chain reaction causes an accident. Jake and Mickey leave the scene, trying to convince themselves they were not involved. The driver of the other car was Luke, a onetime friend of Jake's. Jake struggles to choose the right thing to do. Should he pretend he was not involved and hope Luke doesn't remember? Or should he go to the police?

Also by Eric Walters

Grind

"All I'm saying is that if you took it down a notch or two, you'd make the jumps and save the injuries."

"I always make the jumps," I argued.

"What are you talking about?"

"I make the jumps. It's the landings that I'm having trouble with."

Philip lives for skateboarding. School is merely the break between trying to land a difficult jump and outrunning the security guards. When he and his best friend, Wally, meet a professional skateboarder who videotapes himself for his website, Philip thinks they can do it too—and make money at the same time. When they start getting hits on their website—and making money—they feel the pressure to do more and more dangerous stunts.